Five reasons why you'll love Mirabelle . . .

Mirabelle is magical and mischievous!

Mirabelle is half witch, half fairy, and totally naughty!

She loves making potions with her travelling potion kit!

Mirabelle loves sprinkling a sparkle of mischief wherever she goes!

She has a little baby dragon called Violet!

How do you like to spend time with your grandparents?

We make jam tarts and
I wear a special apron.
– Lyla

I like helping to look after my
nana's cat.
– River

I love having
inside picnics!
– Olivia

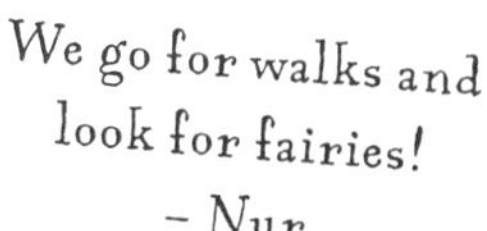

We go for walks and
look for fairies!
– Nur

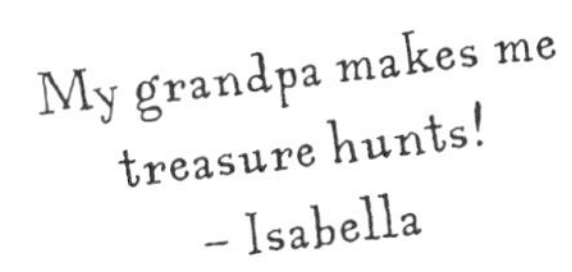

My grandpa makes me
treasure hunts!
– Isabella

They take me on fun trips
like to the library.
– Maryam

My Family
My Mum
Seraphina Starspell
My Dad
Alvin Starspell
Violet

My brother
Wilbur Starspell
Grandpa Starspell
Granny Starspell
Me!
Mirabelle Starspell

Illustrated by Mike Love, based on
original artwork by Harriet Muncaster

OXFORD
UNIVERSITY PRESS

Great Clarendon Street, Oxford OX2 6DP
Oxford University Press is a department of the University of Oxford.
It furthers the University's objective of excellence in research, scholarship,
and education by publishing worldwide. Oxford is a registered trade mark
of Oxford University Press in the UK and in certain other countries

First published in 2022
First published in paperback 2023

British Library Cataloguing in Publication Data

Data available

ISBN: 978-0-19-277758-4

1 3 5 7 9 10 8 6 4 2

Printed in China

Paper used in the production of this book is a natural,
recyclable product made from wood grown in sustainable forests.
The manufacturing process conforms to the environmental
regulations of the country of origin.

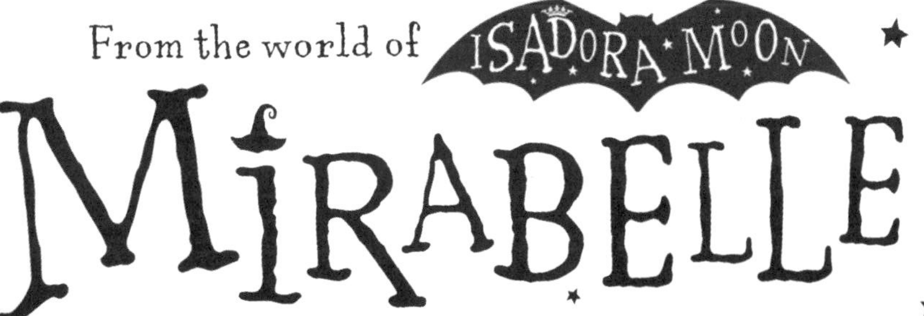

From the world of ISADORA MOON
MIRABELLE
and the Magical Mayhem

Harriet Muncaster

OXFORD
UNIVERSITY PRESS

Chapter ONE

It was the first day of the summer holidays and Wilbur and I were feeling VERY excited. We were on our way to stay with our fairy grandparents—Granny and Grandpa Starspell! It was going to be the first time we had ever stayed at their house without Mum and Dad and it felt like an exciting adventure! Mum

had even bought me a new pair of frog-patterned pyjamas for the occasion. They were folded up neatly in my suitcase which Dad was carrying in his hand as we flew through the sky towards Glimmerview Fairy Village. It was easier for Dad to carry both my and Wilbur's suitcases as

he is a full fairy and has wings! Wilbur and I didn't inherit Dad's fairy wings—we're both more witchy like Mum, so we were both on our broomsticks instead. Suitcases can be awkward to carry on broomsticks as they swing around a lot!

'We're almost there!' said Dad excitedly as the clouds in the sky began to turn a fluffy pink colour like candyfloss and the roads below became empty of cars. Cars are not allowed in Glimmerview Fairy Village.

'Oh look!' cried Dad. 'There's the stream! I used to have such fun playing in the stream with my fairy friends when I was a boy. *Well-behaved* fun of course! We made flower garlands for each other, picked delicious fresh wild fruit, and had swimming races every day in the summer holidays. The sun was *always* shining. Oh, we did have such marvellous times! It was absolutely idyllic!'

Wilbur and I glanced at each other and rolled our eyes. Dad *loves* to go on about the wonderful childhood he had in Glimmerview, surrounded by nature. He also likes to point out that he was a very well-behaved child—unlike me.

'And look,' continued Dad, pointing, 'there's Granny and Grandpa's house!'

'Oh yes!' I said, feeling excitement bubble up inside me again. There it was! A giant toadstool, standing in the middle of a beautiful flowery garden.

Dad landed by the front door of the giant toadstool and Wilbur and I landed next to him. Dad reached out to press the doorbell but before he did, he suddenly

seemed to have second thoughts.

'Mirabelle, Wilbur,' he said, turning round to face us, 'you *do* promise that you will be good at Granny and Grandpa's, don't you?' he asked.

Wilbur looked offended.

'I'm *always* good!' he said indignantly.

'I er . . . was really talking to Mirabelle,' said Dad, staring right into my eyes. 'You do promise to be on your best *fairy* behaviour don't you Mirabelle? You know Granny and Grandpa Starspell don't like mess or mischief, and mess and mischief *do* seem to follow you around!'

'Of *course* I'll be good!' I said to Dad. And I meant it! I really didn't want my lovely fairy grandparents to think badly of me. I was planning to be sweet and helpful and *fairyish.* I was sure being more fairy would impress them!

'And you know they don't like *any*

magic being used without supervision,' said Dad.

'I *know*!' I said, 'I won't do any magic without asking Granny or Grandpa first! I promise!'

'Good,' smiled Dad, looking relieved.

I smiled back feeling only a *tiny* bit guilty. He didn't know that I had put my travelling potion kit into my suitcase. I wasn't planning to *use* it of course! I just liked to have it with me. I have always felt more witch than fairy and I don't like going anywhere without some witch magic—*just in case*! My travelling potion

kit is my lucky charm!

Dad pressed the doorbell and a pretty tinkly tune played out throughout the house. Wilbur and I shuffled impatiently on the doorstep as we heard footsteps coming towards us from inside.

'My sugarplums!' cried Granny when she opened the door. She opened her arms wide and squashed us both into a hug. She smelt of talcum powder and roses and her pale purple hair had been coiffed into neat curls. Grandpa stood next to her, beaming down at Wilbur and me. He was small and neat just like Granny, with a pink pointed beard that had been decorated artfully with stars.

'Come in, come in!' cried Granny. 'Alvin, you will come in for a cup of tea before you fly off won't you?'

'Of course, Mummy,' said Dad. 'Let *me* make it.'

Granny led us into the little kitchen of the toadstool house. As we went through the hallway I smiled as I saw family photographs arranged all over the walls. There was Mum and Dad's wedding photo! And there was one of me with my cousins, Isadora and Honeyblossom.

When we got to the kitchen, we all sat down at the table which was covered with a pretty lacy tablecloth. It looked so clean! I didn't like to touch it just in case I got grubby fingerprints on it. I put my hands in my lap instead and stroked my little pet dragon, Violet, feeling a bit nervous about her making any scorch marks around the house. Violet comes everywhere with me and I have tried very hard to train her to not set things on fire. But sometimes she can't help it if she sneezes or yawns.

Dad put a cup of rose-blossom tea down in front of us all and I sipped mine carefully, being extra careful not to spill any over the side of the cup. Granny and Grandpa sat opposite, asking loads of questions about school. I was just telling them about my teacher, Miss Spindlewick, when I felt something silky brush against my legs.

'Eee!' I squealed, and slopped some of my tea onto the table cloth, leaving a bright pink stain on the spotless lace. Oh no! I felt my cheeks turn bright red.

Dad stared pointedly at me and frowned. He waved his wand to make the stain disappear before Granny and Grandpa noticed. Luckily they were now busy talking to Wilbur about wizard school.

'It was an accident!' I mouthed.

I peered under the table to see who it was who had caused me to spill my tea, and I saw a big fluffy white cat with fairy wings looking up at Violet suspiciously.

'That's Snowspell,' said Granny. 'We adopted her recently. She's quite old. She can't fly any more. She likes to sleep a lot.'

'Hello Snowspell,' I said, reaching out my hand to stroke her. I felt Violet tense on my lap. Violet does not really like it when I pet other animals. She gave a little snort and a couple of purple sparks shot out of her snout, landing on my dress and leaving two tiny black burn marks.

I snatched my hand back up, feeling my throat tighten. *What if the sparks had landed somewhere else in Granny and Grandpa's perfect, pristine house?*

'I think I'll go and unpack my suitcase,' I said hurriedly, sliding off my chair and holding Violet tightly to my chest.

'Me too!' said Wilbur, jumping off his chair and following me. Together we went back out into the hallway and grabbed our suitcases, lugging them all the way upstairs to the bedroom that we were going to have to share. I started to feel excited again. Sometimes it's fun to share a room with someone else. Maybe we would be able to have a midnight feast!

I put my suitcase down on one of the neatly made beds and opened it, getting out my nice new pyjamas and putting

them under my pillow. I put my boring old fairy wand on the bedside table, then I took out my potion kit and stashed it under the bed. Violet fluttered around the room, sniffing at everything. By the time I had unpacked everything, I felt calmer again. The sun was shining through the window. It was a beautiful day! And it was lovely to be here at Granny and Grandpa's house. I was *sure* I could keep out of mischief and be more fairy for a couple of days.

Wilbur and I raced back down the stairs and hugged Dad goodbye. We stood in the garden and waved him off as he fluttered into the sky.

'What would you both like to do now?' asked Granny. 'I wondered if you'd like to go to the stream. Did you bring your swimming costumes?'

'Oh yes!' I cried excitedly.

'Lovely!' said Granny. 'I'll go and pack a picnic!'

Chapter TWO

Soon Granny and Grandpa, Wilbur, and I were on our way to the stream, walking through the golden sunshine and listening to the birds singing in the trees. Butterflies fluttered all about us and flowers waved in the light breeze.

'Isn't it glorious!' said Grandpa. Your dad used to have such fun at the stream

when he was a young boy. Has he ever told you about the wonderful childhood he had growing up in Glimmerview?'

'*Yes,*' said Wilbur and I firmly.

We arrived at the stream and Granny laid out a picnic rug on the bank and set up two deckchairs for her and Grandpa to snooze in, while Wilbur and I got changed into our swimming things. Then we raced into the crystal clear water, splashing each other and laughing. It was such a fun afternoon! Wilbur and I swam until evening, having races and seeing what treasures we could find under the water.

I found a shimmery purple pebble and Wilbur found a rock in the shape of a wizard's hat! Granny and Grandpa watched us from their deckchairs. Then Grandpa had a little sleep and Granny read Good House Magic magazine.

By the time Wilbur and I had finished playing in the water, the sun was beginning to go down, making the pink fluffy clouds above Glimmerview even pinker. Our shadows were long as we walked over to the picnic rug for something to eat. Granny had made some wonderful fairy food! There were cucumber sandwiches, cloud puff biscuits with sugar swirls on top, carrot crisps, and

into our swimming things. Then we raced into the crystal clear water, splashing each other and laughing. It was such a fun afternoon! Wilbur and I swam until evening, having races and seeing what treasures we could find under the water.

I found a shimmery purple pebble and Wilbur found a rock in the shape of a wizard's hat! Granny and Grandpa watched us from their deckchairs. Then Grandpa had a little sleep and Granny read Good House Magic magazine.

By the time Wilbur and I had finished playing in the water, the sun was beginning to go down, making the pink fluffy clouds above Glimmerview even pinker. Our shadows were long as we walked over to the picnic rug for something to eat. Granny had made some wonderful fairy food! There were cucumber sandwiches, cloud puff biscuits with sugar swirls on top, carrot crisps, and

a huge chocolate and cherry cake. After all the playing we had done in the stream, Wilbur and I were very hungry. We ate almost all of the picnic and washed it down with a raspberry crush drink.

'Thank you, Granny!' I said. 'That was delicious. Fairy food is the best!'

'I'm glad you enjoyed it,' said Granny, smiling.

Wilbur and I helped Granny and Grandpa to pack up all the picnic things again and then we walked back to their toadstool house.

'It must be time for bed!' said Granny as she unlocked the front door.

'Oh, already?' asked Wilbur, surprised. 'Mum and Dad usually let Mirabelle and me stay up late during the holidays.'

'Yes,' said Granny, 'but Grandpa and I like to get up at the crack of dawn to see the sunrise. We thought you two might like to join us tomorrow morning? It would be *so* lovely if you did!'

'Oh . . .' I said. 'Umm . . .'

'Of *course* we'll join you Granny!' said Wilbur sweetly. 'Won't we Mirabelle?'

'I . . . guess so.' I replied.

As Wilbur and I walked up the stairs

to our bedroom, I poked him hard with my finger.

'What did you go and agree to that for?' I said. 'Do you know what time the sun rises in summer?'

'I dunno,' said Wilbur. 'It can't be that early, can it?'

'About *four-thirty*,' I told him. 'Four-thirty *a.m.* Wilbur!'

Wilbur looked at me, horrified.

'I can't get up at four-thirty a.m.!' he said. 'That's the middle of the night! I don't believe you!'

'We learned it at school a few weeks ago,' I told him. 'We were doing summer solstice potions.'

Wilbur looked glum.

'Well,' he said. 'We'd really *better* go to bed early then.'

I put on my new frog-patterned pyjamas, brushed my teeth, and climbed into bed. The mattress felt different from my bed at home. It was squashier, like a cloud. It was very comfortable. Just . . . different. It made me feel just the teeniest tiniest bit homesick. Granny and Grandpa came in to kiss us goodnight.

'Sleep well, my sugarplums,' said Granny. 'We'll see you bright and early tomorrow morning! We've set an alarm for you.'

'*We* usually wake up naturally at that

time of course,' said Grandpa. 'But you won't be used to it.'

He set a large silver clock down on the bedside table between Wilbur and me. Wilbur stared at it in dismay.

'Good night!' said Grandpa.

It was hard to get to sleep. Everything felt so different compared to being at home. The noises in the room sounded different, even the air smelt different. I hugged Violet to me tightly and lit my wand so that I could read one of my favourite books about a tinsel-haired witch. It was comforting and familiar. It made me feel less homesick.

Books really are a kind of magic, I thought as I drifted away into sleep.

BRINNNNG!!! BRINNNNNNG!!! went the alarm at four-thirty the next morning.

Wilbur shot up in bed.

'Wha—what's happening?!' he yelped, confused.

I reached out my hand and slammed the top of the alarm clock, trying to turn it off in the darkness. It fell to the floor with a clatter.

'Oops,' I said, properly awake now.

'Rise and shine!' came Granny's sing-song voice, as she burst into the bedroom. 'Time to watch the sunrise. There's nothing more beautiful than watching nature do its thing!'

I dragged myself out of bed and threw my dressing gown on over my pyjamas. Wilbur did the same. Together we followed Granny and Grandpa out of the toadstool house and into the garden. There was a calm quiet chill in the early morning air.

'I've got you both a pair of enchanted fairy wings to wear,' said Grandpa, holding out two pairs of lilac sparkly wings. 'There's nothing more exhilarating than swooping and soaring through the air in front of the rising sun.'

'Oh thank you, Grandpa!' I said, suddenly feeling much more excited about our early morning activity. I took the wings and put them on, feeling them flutter gently against my back. The last time I had worn enchanted fairy wings was when I was a bridesmaid at my Aunt Crystal's wedding but that was ages ago! I was excited to try them again.

'Look at me, Wilbur!' I yelled as I flapped up into the air.

Wilbur looked up at me, clutching his wings. He looked embarrassed.

'Uh, wizards don't really wear fairy wings, Grandpa,' he said. 'It's just not very . . . wizardy.'

'Oh don't be silly Wilbur!' said Grandpa, fluttering into the air now on his own, real fairy wings. 'You're half fairy too, don't forget!'

'I suppose,' mumbled Wilbur. Reluctantly he put the wings on and joined us in the sky. Together the four of us wheeled through the air, dancing and diving on the breeze, our wings fluttering behind us. Then the sun began to rise, bathing us in a golden syrupy glow. It felt very magical. *I* felt magical!

'Nature really *can* be very special!' I thought.

When we had finished our sunrise flight, we all went back into the toadstool house for breakfast. I felt very hungry after all the energy I had used up that morning. Granny made us fairy cloud pancakes which we ate with whipped cream and strawberries. They were delicious!

'What would you like to do today?' asked Granny.

'Sleep!' yawned Wilbur.

'Can we go to the stream again?' I asked.

'Of course!' said Granny. 'We'll go a bit later. I just have to pop into the village to do a few errands first. Do you want to come?'

'That's OK Granny,' said Wilbur quickly. 'I think I might go back to bed for a bit.'

'I'll come,' I said, not wanting Granny to feel disappointed, even though I would have quite liked to go back to bed too. Being polite was turning out to be rather exhausting!

Chapter THREE

Wilbur and I helped to clear away the breakfast things and then Granny and I left the toadstool house to go to town. It was another beautiful day in fairyland, and the birds chirped, butterflies fluttered and the sun shone as we made our way towards the shops. It was really quite cheering and Violet flapped along happily beside my ear as we walked.

'Here we are!' said Granny, leading me into a fairy bakery where puffs of pink flour wafted out of the door. It smelt lovely inside and there was a whole counter of delicious-looking cakes and

pastries. Granny let me choose some to take home. I picked an iced cherry bun for me and a strawberry swirl slice for Wilbur. Then she has a long chat with the baker which was a bit boring.

Next, we went to the grocer's stall which was in the market outside. Granny piled up a basket with provisions.

'Ooh this is getting heavy!' she remarked.

'Do you need me to carry it for you?' I asked, hoping that she would say no.

'Oh, if you don't mind Mirabelle!' said Granny. 'You *are* kind!'

She handed me the basket and I took it, feeling pleased that Granny thought I was kind. I was being much more helpful than *Wilbur*. Then Granny had a long chat with the grocer about the weather and the shortage of fairy dust at the moment. I stood there as patiently as I could, trying

not to tap my foot on the ground or yawn because that would be rude. Were some people this good and helpful all the time? How did they do it?!

After the grocers, we had to go to the haberdashery where Granny picked out a ball of rainbow wool and then after that, the pharmacy where Granny bought some peppermint tablets for Grandpa's indigestion. I followed her, lugging the heavy bags and waiting while Granny

chatted to all the shopkeepers. She seemed to know *everyone* in Glimmerview!

I was quite relieved when we were finally finished and it was time to go home. The bags were feeling very heavy now and I was extra tired from having to get up so early that morning. I felt like if I had to be polite and helpful and *fairy-ish* for much longer, I might explode.

'I think I might go and have a little nap,' I said when we got back to the toadstool house.

'Good idea!' said Grandpa, who had been busy doing a crossword at the kitchen table. 'I think I'll go and have a little nap too,' and he disappeared off

to the sitting room with his newspaper. I left Granny unpacking the shopping and ran up the stairs with Violet sitting on my shoulder. It felt nice to be on my own again for a bit. I felt like I could BREATHE again.

I reached the bedroom, expecting to see Wilbur in there, but his bed was empty. He must have finished his snooze and gone to do something else. But there was someone else in our room. Curled up in the middle of my pillow was Snowspell!

'Oh dear,' I thought as I felt Violet stiffen on my shoulder. I reached up to pet her but before I could, she fluttered

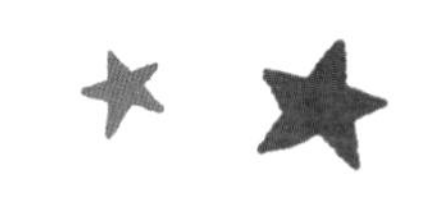

up into the air and blew a little flame of fire towards the bed. It landed right next to Snowspell who immediately jumped up with a yowl and stalked out of the room, shooting an evil glare towards us.

'Violet!' I exclaimed. 'That was naughty!'

Violet ignored me and flew over to the bed where she settled down in the warm spot that Snowspell had made on my pillow.

I stared in dismay at the bed. There was now a small round scorch mark on the flower-patterned duvet. It looked awful! My heart started to pitter-patter. What would Granny and Grandpa think?

'Violet!' I said again, feeling cross.

I had tried so hard to be good and kind, keeping everything tidy in Granny and Grandpa's nice neat house so far, and now Violet had ruined it all!

I stood there for a few moments, thinking about what to do. I could magic it away with my fairy wand, but I didn't know exactly where it was. I had left it downstairs somewhere after we had been on the picnic yesterday. I didn't want to risk leaving the bedroom in case someone came in and saw the scorch mark, Wilbur would tell tales on me, I knew it!

I hurried over to the bedroom door and closed it gently, an idea beginning to form in my mind. I knew how to get rid of stains with my witch magic too! I could do a quick little potion to fix the duvet and no one would ever know! I had promised Dad that I wouldn't use my witch magic, or *any* magic, without Granny and Grandpa's permission, but this was an emergency!

My fingertips began to tingle. Now I had thought of it, the idea was irresistible.

I rummaged under my bed for my travelling potion kit, pulling it out, and gazing at it lovingly. I had missed feeling witchy over the last couple of days. I had been acting more fairy as I was sure being more fairy would please Granny and Grandpa but now it felt like the real me was bursting to get out. I would feel much better if I could just do a *little* bit of witch magic in secret. Then it would be *much* easier to keep being good, polite, and fairylike afterwards.

I pulled my tiny cauldron towards me and began to open some of the miniature glass bottles. They were full of all sorts of ingredients. There was powdered bat's claw, crow feathers, beetle wings, toadstool spots, and some glowing starshine. We had learnt the stain-removing spell at school quite recently. I was *sure* I remembered it.

Carefully I poured a little of the starshine into my cauldron, watching how it shimmered like a cloudy mist. What came next? Oh yes, three toadstool spots! Or was it four? I had better put in four just to be safe. What next? A pinch of beetle wings . . . and then a thimbleful of powdered bat's claw. Or was it supposed to be a *sprinkling*? I couldn't quite remember but surely it wouldn't make much difference. I stirred all the ingredients together, watching how the potion glittered and twinkled in the cauldron. It looked lovely! Like a sort of purple shimmery sparkly goo. That *was* how it was supposed to look, wasn't it?

I scooped out some of the potion and hurried over to my bed, smoothing it onto the scorch mark. I stood back, watching and waiting, expecting it to start fading immediately.

But nothing seemed to happen.

Although . . . I peered closer. Was the scorch mark actually getting bigger?

No, surely not.

But . . .

Maybe it was!

I started to feel quite panicked as I watched the scorch mark begin to grow.

'Stop!' I ordered it. 'Stop!'

But the mark just grew and grew until it was almost the size of the duvet!

I must have done the potion wrong!

Maybe I had put in too much powdered bat's claw? Or had I added too many toadstool spots? Now that I thought about it, hadn't the potion that we had made at school been green, not purple?

I stared at my burnt-looking duvet in horror. How in the name of leaping frogs was I going to fix it now?! Maybe I should try and make the potion again? Maybe I was supposed to put a crow feather into it. Yes, that must be it! I had forgotten the crow feather!

I knelt on the carpet and began to mix up the potion again. But it was hard to concentrate. I felt so worried and my hands were all shaky. What would

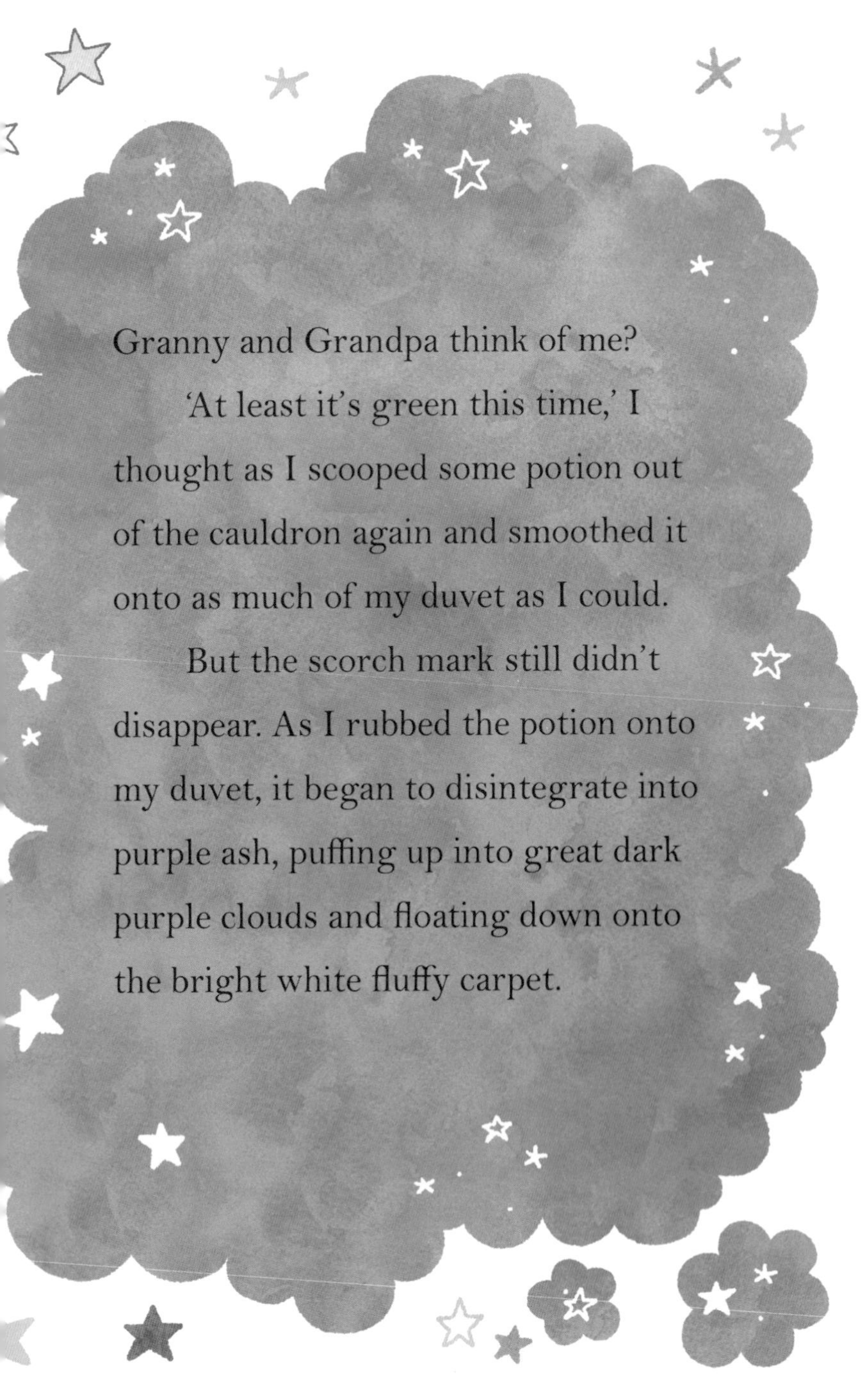

Granny and Grandpa think of me?

'At least it's green this time,' I thought as I scooped some potion out of the cauldron again and smoothed it onto as much of my duvet as I could.

But the scorch mark still didn't disappear. As I rubbed the potion onto my duvet, it began to disintegrate into purple ash, puffing up into great dark purple clouds and floating down onto the bright white fluffy carpet.

I felt sick.

What had I done?

Maybe my fairy wand would help? Somehow I would have to get hold of it!

I shoved all my potion ingredients back under the bed and opened the bedroom door, peeping out to check that no one was on the landing. The coast was clear! I scooted out of the room and hurried down the stairs as fast as I could, trailing my hand down the banister. Where had I left my wand? Was it in the sitting room? I peered in. Grandpa was asleep but Granny was sitting there knitting with her new ball of rainbow-coloured wool. My wand was on the coffee

table right in front of her. There was no way I could go in and get it while she was there! She would ask me what I needed it for! Magic was supposed to be *supervised* in Granny and Grandpa's house.

I backed away from the open sitting-room door before Granny could spot me. And then I saw something else.

'Oh my stars!' I whispered, putting my hand over my mouth.

A trail of sooty purple footprints led down the hallway. As I crept back along it, I saw that they went all the way up the stairs too and the bannister rail was all grubby. I looked at my hands. They were covered in purple soot and ash. I peered into the mirror. There were smudges of purple all over my face! *And* all over my clothes!

This was bad. This was really bad! This was turning into a *nightmare*!

There was only one thing for it.

I would have to ask Wilbur for help!

But where was he?!

He wasn't upstairs and I couldn't hear him anywhere in the house downstairs.

He must be in the garden.

I hurried outside into the sunshine.

'Wilbur!' I called. 'Wilbur! Where are you?'

'Uh!' came Wilbur's voice from behind the shed. 'Mirabelle is that you?'

'Yes, it's me!' I said, relieved to have found him.

Wilbur's head popped out from behind the shed. he looked flushed and worried.

'Er,' he said. 'Don't come behind here.'

'Why?' I asked, frowning.

I immediately ran to look behind the shed.

'Don't look, Mirabelle, don't look!' he yelped.

I looked.

'Wilbur!' I exclaimed. Because what I saw made my heart sink but also soar at the same time.

We were going to be in so much trouble.

But at least we were going to be in trouble *together.*

Wilbur had been using wizard magic.

Chapter FOUR

I could tell Wilbur had been using wizard magic because his fingertips were slightly sparking. Wizards use their hands a lot to do magic. In front of him sat Snowspell the cat. But she didn't look quite like she usually does. Her snowy white fur had turned bright purple and her usually dormant wings were fluttering. They kept lifting her a few inches up off the ground, before plonking her back down again. She looked completely bewildered.

'Mirabelle, don't tell Granny and Grandpa!' said Wilbur, twisting his hands about worriedly. 'I just couldn't resist doing some magic. But it all went a bit wrong! I was only trying to do something nice for Snowspell. She came out into the garden looking so cross!'

'Ah,' I said. 'Well, I think I know why . . .'

'I thought she might cheer up if I could make her fly properly for a bit,' said Wilbur, 'like she would have been able to when she was a kitten! But it didn't work how it was supposed to, and for some reason she turned purple too!'

Snowspell lifted jerkily back up into

the air again for a few moments, before juddering back down to the ground. She gave a confused 'mew'.

'I feel so bad!' said Wilbur. 'I don't know how to fix it with wizard magic. I already tried. Have you got your fairy wand with you? I think mine's fallen down the side of the chair that Grandpa's sitting on!'

'Oh!' I said, my heart sinking. 'Wilbur, I was hoping you'd have your fairy wand on you. 'I have a little problem of my own . . .'

I told Wilbur everything that had happened back up in our bedroom. Wilbur stared at me in dismay but I could also tell that he was glad he wasn't the only one to do something wrong.

'I didn't mean to make so much mess,' I finished. 'Everything just got a bit out of control. You won't tell on me will you Wilbur?'

'As long as *you* don't tell on *me*,' replied Wilbur.

'It's a pact!' I said and we shook hands on it.

'What now then?' asked Wilbur. 'We have to see if we can sort it out before Granny and Grandpa see. They'll be *so* cross! They hate mess!'

'I'm sure if we both work together with your wizard magic and my witch magic, we can fix everything!' I said hopefully. 'I'll try and fix Snowspell and you can fix my duvet. Let's go back into the house. My witch kit is in our bedroom!'

I picked up Snowspell and carried her

towards the house. Wilbur and I snuck past the sitting-room door and hurried up the stairs to our bedroom. I put Snowspell down and she immediately jumped onto my bed, pawing at all the purple ash that was on there. It puffed up in more clouds, putting stains on the walls and ceiling.

'Use your wizard magic to help, Wilbur!' I said. 'Please!'

'OK,' said Wilbur, rolling up his sleeves self-importantly. 'We did stain-removing potions last term at school.'

'Wait!' I said, lifting Snowspell off the bed and plonking her down on the floor. It wouldn't do for her to get in the firing line of Wilbur's spell.

'Ready?' said Wilbur.

'Yes,' I nodded. I really, really hoped that Wilbur knew what he was doing. Sometimes he's a *little* overconfident about what he can do with wizard magic. But what was the worst that could happen now?

'Good,' said Wilbur, 'I'll need *complete* silence. Wizard magic is very sensitive.'

I rolled my eyes.

Wilbur held his hands out over my bed and wiggled his fingers.

'Riddlydiddlyponk!' he shouted.

I tried not to snigger. Sometimes wizard magic can sound a bit silly. Witch magic is much more glamorous!

Sparks shot out of Wilbur's fingers and landed all over my bed and the walls and the ceiling around it. There was a fizzing and a POOF and then . . .

'Oh my stars!' I whispered.

Wilbur opened his eyes.

'Oh,' he said, frowning.

I didn't think things could get worse.

But they just had.

'Wilbur!' I wailed. 'You haven't just made the mess disappear. You've made *everything* disappear!'

'Ah, ahem, yes well . . .' said Wilbur, frowning. 'You must have breathed too loudly. I *did* say wizard magic is very sensitive.'

I stared round in dismay. My bed had completely disappeared and so had everything underneath it. All we could see was bare carpet.

'My witch kit!' I said suddenly. 'It's gone! How am I supposed to help you fix Snowspell without my witch kit?'

Wilbur's face turned grey.

'Do some more wizard magic!' I said. 'Make everything come back!'

'Uh!' said Wilbur, scratching his head.

‘I’m not sure if we should—’

Just then there was the sound of footsteps coming up the stairs. Both Wilbur and I froze, staring at each other in horror.

It was too late. We’d missed our chance to fix things!

Granny or Grandpa were going to see what we'd done! They were going to be so cross!

'Mirabelle?' came a voice from outside the door. 'Wilbur?'

The door handle turned and Granny's head popped into the room.

'Granny!' I squeaked.

Granny peered into the room. Her mouth fell open as she looked at the bare place on the carpet where my bed had been and at Snowspell who was fluttering up in the air above Wilbur's bed. Her eyes went very, very round.

'What in the name of twinkling toadstools has been going on?' she asked.

'Oh, Granny!' I cried, bursting into tears. 'I'm so sorry! It was all a big mistake! Violet made a scorch mark on the nice clean duvet and I tried to fix it with witch magic so that I woudn't have to bother you, but it all went wrong!'

'I just wanted to do something nice for Snowspell,' muttered Wilbur. 'But I shouldn't have been using magic without asking you. I'm sorry Granny.'

Granny looked at us both.

She narrowed her eyes.

She looked at Snowspell.

She put her hands on her hips.

I waited for her to tell us off.

But then . . . she just shook her head

and laughed!

'You two are just like your father,' she said.

'Dad!?' scoffed Wilbur. 'Dad would never make a mess like this!'

'Dad always tells us stories about how *good* he was growing up!' I added.

'He was good,' said Granny, stepping into the room now, '*most* of the time. But he definitely had a cheeky streak! I remember one time when he couldn't be

bothered to run an errand for me and go to the shop to get butter. He tried to magic it up instead but he wasn't very good with his wand at that point. Our house was filled with yellow butterflies for a whole week!'

'Oh!' said both Wilbur and me in surprise.

'Yes,' smiled Granny. 'Anyway, we ought to sort all this mess out. Where are your wands? Let's do it together, it will be good practice for you.'

Chapter FIVE

I went downstairs and retrieved both my and Wilbur's wands from the sitting room. I even managed to reach my hand down the side of Grandpa's chair to fetch Wilbur's without waking him up! I raced back upstairs.

'Now!' said Granny. 'Let's start with the carpet, shall we? It's a bit mucky!'

We all gazed down at the once spotless white carpet which was now covered all over with dark purple smudges. Granny waved her wand and there was a flurry of sparks.

'Much better!' she said. 'It was time for a change anyway!'

Instead of a spotless white carpet, we now found ourselves standing on a squashy dark purple one with black stars all over it.

'And while we're at it,' continued Granny, 'it might be time to change the walls too.' She waved her wand at the flowery pastel-coloured walls. In another flurry of sparks, they become covered in lovely black and purple cat wallpaper.

'Oh, I love the new wallpaper Granny!' I said.

'I thought it would make you feel at home,' smiled Granny. 'I do know you feel

a bit more witch than fairy most of the time!'

'You do?' I asked.

'Of course!' said Granny. 'I think you've been trying to hide your witch side over the last couple of days to please Grandpa and me. Mirabelle, you must

never try and hide who you are just to fit in with who you think other people might want you to be.'

I looked down at the floor, feeling a bit foolish.

'We love you for who you are!' said Granny. 'Being half witch is what makes you you!'

'So you don't mind if I do witch magic while I'm here then?' I asked hopefully.

'That's not what I meant,' smiled Granny, ruffling my hair. 'I'd just like you to ask permission before you do *any* sort of magic in my house. Otherwise,' she gestured towards Snowspell, 'we get into messes like this! I don't mind if you make a mess if it's an accident. Just tell me and I'll come and help to sort it out!'

Wilbur and I glanced at each other, a bit embarrassed.

'And now for Snowspell,' said Granny. 'I'm not sure she suits purple! You try to change her back, Mirabelle.'

I closed my eyes and waved my wand

over the big fluffy cat, imagining her to be snowy white as she was before. A shower of sparks rained down over her.

'Almost,' said Granny. When I opened my eyes I saw that Snowspell was now stripy.

'Let me try,' said Wilbur. He waved his fairy wand and this time Snowspell turned fully white and her wings stopped flapping. She landed gently on Wilbur's bed where she promptly curled up and went to sleep.

'Lovely!' said Granny. 'What next. 'Oh, I know, the bed! Mirabelle, you can make it appear again!'

'Can I?' I said hesitantly. I felt a bit unsure about my ability to do fairy magic—I don't often use my fairy wand.

'*I* believe you can!' said Granny.

I closed my eyes tight once again and imagined my bed to be back where it was with my witch kit underneath it. It felt a bit easier this time, with Granny cheering me on.

'Not *quite* the same duvet as you had before,' said Granny, when I opened my eyes. 'But maybe it suits the room better now.'

Instead of the pastel-coloured flowery duvet, there was a black and purple striped one.

'I want a black and purple striped duvet!' said Wilbur. 'Can I magic mine Granny?'

'I don't see why not,' said Granny.

Once everything in the room was back in order Granny fetched some fairy dust, and Wilbur and I sprinkled it all over the stairs and down the banister rail to get rid of the footprints and handprint stains. Once we were finished Granny and Grandpa's house looked just like it had before. Spotless.

‘Well done Mirabelle and Wilbur,’ said Granny. Then she held out her hand for our wands.

‘I think I’ll look after these for the rest of the visit,’ she said. ‘And your witch kit too Mirabelle. I don’t want you doing any more magic without asking first.’

‘OK Granny,’ I smiled. I really didn’t mind and I don’t think Wilbur did either. What did we need our wands for anyway? Next time I would speak to Granny and Grandpa first if there was a problem.

Once Wilbur and I had given our wands to Granny and I had scrabbled under the bed for my witch kit, we both helped to make a rather late lunch.

After everything that had happened, I found that I didn't feel quite so nervous about making a mess. I happily chopped up tomatoes, (even though some of the juice did spurt on the floor) while Wilbur buttered some bread.

'Ah! That was a long nap!' said Grandpa as he came into the kitchen. 'What's been going on while I've been dozing then, eh?'

He ruffled Wilbur's hair and Wilbur looked at me. I looked at Granny and Granny smiled.

'We had a bit of a magical mishap,' she said. 'But it's all fine now. Nothing to bother yourself with dear!'

Grandpa nodded, unfazed.

'I could do with a nice hearty lunch,' he said. 'And then we can go to the stream! I've had such a long nap I feel energized for a swim this afternoon.'

'Oh yeah!' said Wilbur. 'We can play chase Grandpa!'

'You'll never catch me!' winked Grandpa.

That afternoon we had such a lovely time at the stream that I forgot all

about the worry and panic from earlier. Grandpa came into the water with us and we splashed about like little fish.

Even Granny decided to come in for a bit! Then Granny and Grandpa took us out to Fairy Bites—a restaurant in the village that served delicious pizzas. When we got home afterwards, I decided to be honest and told Granny and Grandpa that I didn't want to get up at four-thirty a.m. again. It had been nice the first time but I really needed my sleep! They didn't seem to mind at all!

The following day Mum and Dad came to pick us up.

'Have you had a lovely time?' they asked.

'Have you been *good*?' asked Dad, suspiciously.

'Well . . .' I began.

'They've been *wonderful*!' beamed Granny, winking at me. 'We've absolutely loved having Mirabelle and Wilbur. They've really brightened the place up! They're welcome to come and stay any time!'

I gave Granny a huge squishy hug and then gave Grandpa one too.

'Thank you for having me!' I said.

'You're very welcome,' said Granny. And then she slipped something into my hand when Mum and Dad weren't looking. It was a tiny witchy spell book.

'I found it in the Glimmerview junk shop,' said Granny. 'Thought you'd like it for your doll's house!'

I felt a warm glow travel all the way down from my head to my toes.

'Thank you, Granny!' I beamed.

I gazed down at the tiny book and then looked back up at Granny.

'You know what else I need for my doll's house?' I said. 'A tiny, fairy magic wand! Maybe I can look for one in the junk shop next time I visit? Or we could make one together?'

Granny looked delighted.

'Of course we can!' she said.

I stood on tiptoe so that I could

whisper in her ear.

'I think I'm more like you and Dad than I realized,' I said. 'A bit more fairy than I thought!'

Granny winked at me.

'I won't tell anyone!' she promised and her eyes twinkled mischievously.

I grinned.

'Goodbye, Granny.'

'Goodbye, Mirabelle.' She replied. 'My little witch fairy.'

Quiz

Are you more witch or more fairy?
Take the quiz to find out!

What is your favourite time of day?

A. Early in the morning.

B. Late at night.

2. How tidy is your bedroom?

A. Very tidy!

B. It's pretty messy.

3. Last time you went shopping did you help to carry the bags?

A. Of course!

B. No—they're so heavy!

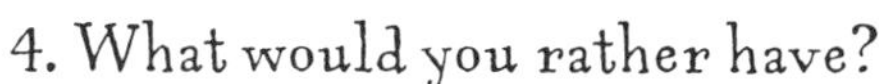

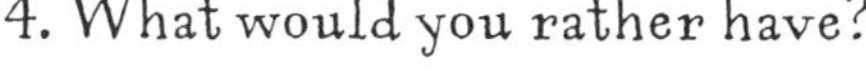

4. What would you rather have?

A. A wand.

B. A potion kit.

Results

Mostly As

You are a fairy at heart! With your tidy and helpful nature you would fit right in at Granny and Grandpa Starspell's toadstool house.

Mostly Bs

You are a witch! You love staying up late and thinking of potions to invent, you're far too busy to be tidy!

A mixture of As and Bs

Just like Mirabelle and Wilbur, you're a bit of both! With a winning combination of fairy and witch qualities, you'd be right at home in Mirabelle's magical world.

To visit Harriet Muncaster's
website, visit
harrietmuncaster.co.uk

Harriet Muncaster, that's me! I'm the author and illustrator of two young fiction series, Mirabelle and Isadora Moon. I love anything teeny tiny, anything starry, and everything glittery.

ISADORA MOON

ISADORA MOON
Has a Sleepover
Half vampire, half fairy, totally unique!
Harriet Muncaster

ISADORA MOON
Puts on a Show
Half vampire, half fairy, totally unique!
Harriet Muncaster

ISADORA MOON
Goes on Holiday
Half vampire, half fairy, totally unique!
Harriet Muncaster

ISADORA MOON
Goes to a Wedding
Half vampire, half fairy, totally unique!
Harriet Muncaster

ISADORA MOON
Meets the Tooth Fairy
Half vampire, half fairy, totally unique!
Harriet Muncaster

ISADORA MOON
and the Shooting Star
Half vampire, half fairy, totally unique!
Harriet Muncaster

ISADORA MOON
Gets the Magic Pox
Half vampire, half fairy, totally unique!
Harriet Muncaster

ISADORA MOON
Under the Sea
Half vampire, half fairy, totally unique!
Harriet Muncaster

ISADORA MOON
and the New Girl
Half vampire, half fairy, totally unique!
Harriet Muncaster

More mischievous stories to collect

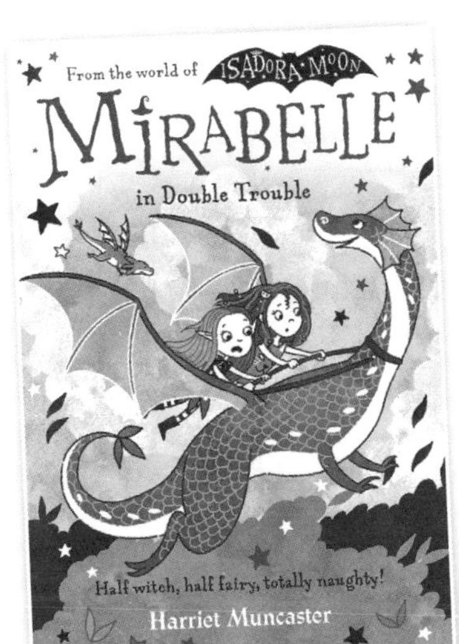
From the world of
ISADORA MOON
MIRABELLE
in Double Trouble
Half witch, half fairy, totally naughty!
Harriet Muncaster

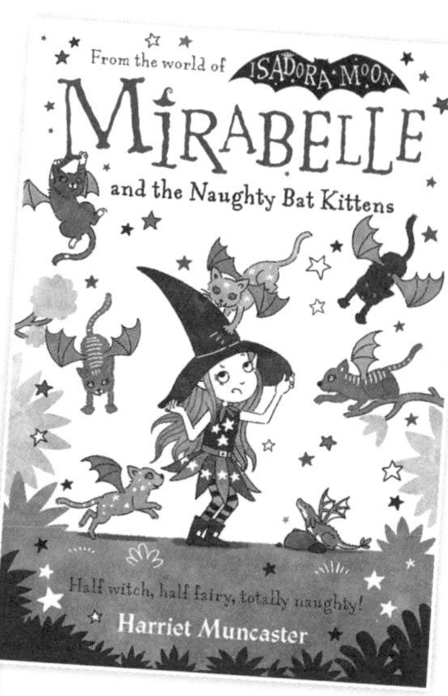
From the world of
ISADORA MOON
MIRABELLE
and the Naughty Bat Kittens
Half witch, half fairy, totally naughty!
Harriet Muncaster

From the world of
ISADORA MOON
MIRABELLE
and the Magical Mayhem
Half witch, half fairy, totally naughty!
Harriet Muncaster

From the world of
ISADORA MOON
MIRABELLE
Takes Charge
Half witch, half fairy, totally naughty!
Harriet Muncaster

Get ready to meet Isadora's mermaid friend, Emerald!

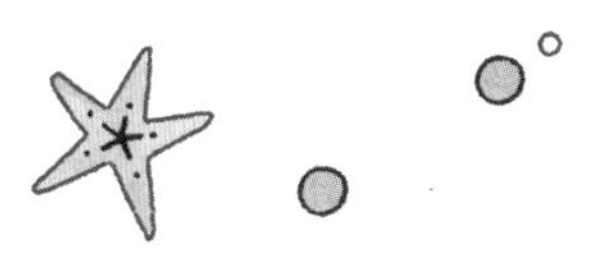

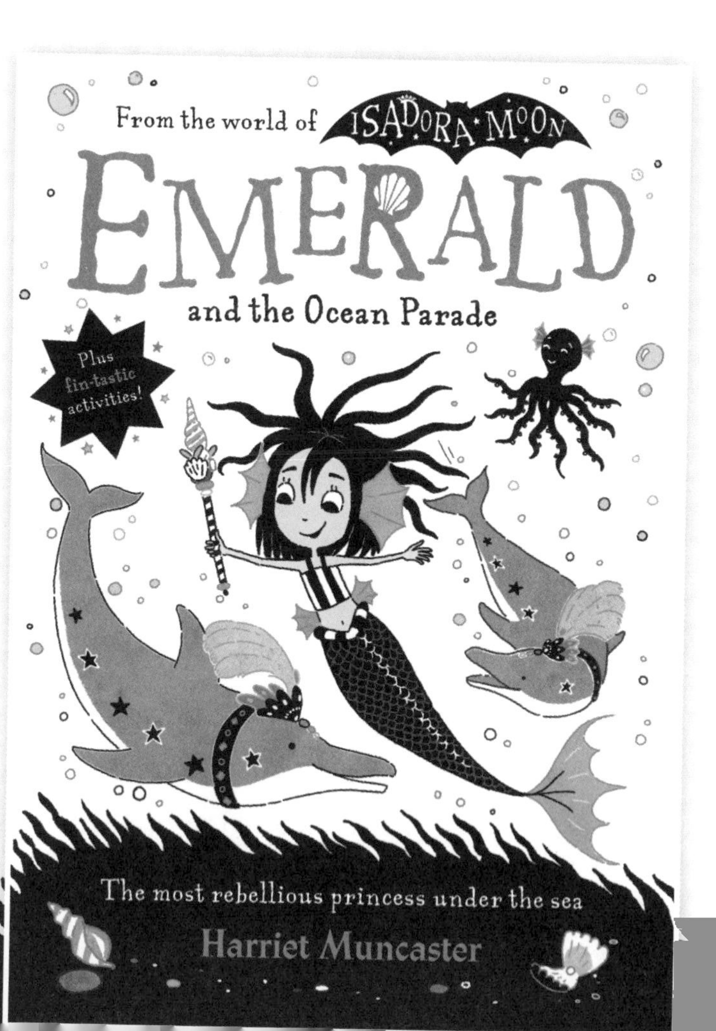
From the world of ISADORA MOON
EMERALD
and the Ocean Parade
Plus fin-tastic activities!
The most rebellious princess under the sea
Harriet Muncaster

Like Mirabelle? Why not try . . .